The Dumb Bunnies

Story by Sue Denim · Pictures by Dav Pilkey

SCHOLASTIC INC. · NEW YORK TORONTO LONDON AUCKLAND SYDNEY

FOR JAMES MARSHALL

Special thanks to Thacher Hurd and the folks
at HarperCollins for letting the Dumb Bunnies
spend the night in the Good Night Moon Room.

ISBN 0-590-22968-0

Text copyright © 1994 by Sue Denim
Illustrations copyright © 1994 by Dav Pilkey
All rights reserved. Published by Scholastic Inc.

12 11 10 9 8 7 6 5 4 3 2 1   3   5 6 7 8 9/9 0/0

Printed in the United States of America   14

Original Blue Sky Press edition designed by Dav Pilkey
and Kathleen Westray

Once upon a time there were three dumb bunnies who lived in a log cabin made out of bricks.

Momma Bunny was really dumb.
Poppa Bunny was even dumber.

And Baby Bunny was the dumbest bunny of all.

One day, the Dumb Bunnies were eating their porridge.

Momma Bunny's porridge was too cold, so she blew on it.

Poppa Bunny's porridge was too hot, so he put it in the oven.

But Baby Bunny's porridge was just right,
so he poured it down his pants.
"That's my boy!" said Poppa Bunny.

The Dumb Bunnies decided to go to
town and finish their porridge later.
"Should we drive, or should we take
our bikes?" asked Poppa Bunny.

So they took their bikes.

"Can I drive the car?" asked Baby Bunny.
"You don't know how to drive," said Poppa
Bunny. "You'd get us all killed."
"Aw, please?" asked Baby Bunny.
"Duh, okay," said Poppa Bunny.

When the Dumb Bunnies finally got to town,
they had a marvelous time.

They went ice-skating at the lake.

They bowled a home run at the public library.

And they had a nice picnic lunch
at the car wash.

Meanwhile, back at the Dumb Bunnies' house, a little girl came skipping up the sidewalk.
The little girl had *very* white skin.
Her skin was as white as snow.
In fact, her skin was so snowy white that everybody called her...

...Little Red Goldilocks (although nobody was quite sure why).

Little Red Goldilocks broke into the Dumb Bunnies' house and made herself right at home.

When the Dumb Bunnies returned, they knew something was not right.

"Somebody's been sleeping in my porridge," said Poppa Bunny.

"Somebody's been eating my bed,"
said Momma Bunny.

"And somebody's been using my pimple cream," cried Baby Bunny.

Suddenly, the Dumb Bunnies saw the intruder.
"My name is Little Red Goldilocks," she said.
"I have beautiful golden locks!"
"Duh, yeah," said Poppa Bunny, "and you have nice yellow hair, too."

The Dumb Bunnies *loved* Little Red Goldilocks.
Poppa Bunny loved her so much, he danced
a merry dance.

Momma Bunny loved her so much,
she sang a merry song.

And Baby Bunny loved her so much...

...he flushed her down the merry toilet.

"That's my boy!" said Poppa Bunny.

Finally, the Dumb Bunnies returned to their porridge, which by now was *just* the right temperature.

So they poured it on their heads...

...and lived happily ever after.